AF504389

Lucky meets Tony the Pony

Lucky s Big Adventure series

By: Brian Stewart

Published by Book Writing Pioneer
Cover design by Book Writing Pioneer
ISBN: Printed in the United States

Preface
(from the Author)

Welcome, to the, Lucky Big Adventure Series
Thank you for your purchase. This book was written to help young children and their parents or readers to have talking points and situations to discuss acceptance. Every character in this story has a function in life, their own passion, hopes, and dreams. At the end of each page, there is an opportunity to discuss and learn about acceptance of others and their own personnel needs. We all have gifts we like to share with others, but we all have our own needs and desires. Understanding and accepting others for who and what they are is a learned behavior.

Again, Thank you
Brian Stewart

Lucky Big Adventure Books:

Lucky Gets A Pony
Lucky Saves The Circus
Lucky Goes To The Derby
Lucky Saves Christmas
Lucky Learns To Skate

LUCKY IS A YOUNG CHILD LIKE YOU.
HE IS ALWAYS LOOKING FOR
SOMETHING TO DO.
HE LOVES TO PLAY WITH HIS
BEAGLE NAMED DAISY.
THEY RUN THROUGH THE YARD,
AND BOTH ACT CRAZY.

DAISY LOVES TO RUN RABBITS
AND CHASE THEM AWAY.
SHE LEAVES LUCKY ALL
ALONE, WITH NO ONE TO
PLAY.
SHE IS PROTECTING THE
GARDEN, KEEPING RABBITS
AT BAY.

POOR LUCKY, HE SITS WITH
NOTHING TO DO.
"I WISH I HAD SOME FRIENDS,
MAYBE ONE OR TWO."
"IF I HAD SOME FRIENDS, I'D
HAVE SOMETHING TO DO."

"I'LL GO NEXT DOOR AND SEE WHAT FARMER ED IS DOING."
"HELLO, FARMER ED, WHAT IS THAT LITTLE GOAT CHEWING?"
"TOAT IS A GOAT: HE LIKES TO CHEW ON EVERYTHING HE SEES."
"TOAT WILL CLEAN UP YOUR FARM, EATING BUSHES AND TREES."

"CAN I BORROW TOAT?"
"TO LET HIM EAT SOME OF OUR BUSHES AND TREES?..
"I'VE NOTHING TO DO. CAN I BORROW TOAT, CAN I, PRETTY PLEASE?..
"SURE YOU CAN, LUCKY, IT'LL GIVE YOU SOME-THING TO DO...
"JUST BE CAREFUL WHERE YOU TAKE HIM: HE'LL EVEN EAT YOUR SHOE...

"WHEN YOU BRING HIM BACK, PUT HIM IN
HIS STABLE...
"WITH EINSWINE, THE PIG, WITH SOME
SWEET CORN, IF YOU'RE ABLE...

LUCKY WAS HOPING THAT TOAT WOULD BE SO MUCH FUN.
LUCKY TIED HIM TO A TREE SO AWAY HE COULDN'T RUN.
LUCKY SOON FOUND OUT THAT TOAT WASN'T VERY MUCH FUN.
TOAT JUST ATE BUSHES AND TREES: WOULD HE EVER GET DONE?

LUCKY TOOK TOAT BACK TO FARMER ED'S BARN AT THE END OF THE DAY.
LUCKY WAS DISAPPOINTED BECAUSE TOAT DIDN'T WANT TO PLAY.
FARMER ED ASKED, "HAVE YOU MET EINSWINE? HE IS SUCH A GOOD PIG?..
"HE WILL TURN OVER YOUR GARDEN, WITH HIS SNOOT, FOR ROOTS HE WILL DIG.

LUCKY WALKED EINSWINE HOME AND PUT HIM IN THE GARDEN TO PLOW. HE WATCHED EINSWINE DIG AND ROOT. AND IT WAS ONLY FUN FOR A WHILE.

FARMER ED ASKED LUCKY, "WHY ARE YOU WEARING A FROWN?"
"TELL ME YOUR TROUBLES. TELL ME WHAT HAS GOT YOU DOWN?"

"DAISY WOULD RATHER HAVE A RABBIT TO RUN.
THEN PLAY WITH ME AND HAVE SOME FUN.."
"TOAT WANTS TO EAT A BUSH OR A TREE.
NO TIME TO PLAY OR RUN WITH ME, YOU SEE.
EINSWINE, THE PIG, JUST WANTS TO DIG ALL DAY.
HE WON'T DANCE OR RUN: HE JUST DIGS EVERY DAY.
THEY HAVE THEIR OWN THINGS THAT THEY LIKE TO DO.
I WANT THEM TO BE HAPPY: I LOVE THE WHOLE CREW.
NOW I NEED A PAL: I NEED SOMETHING TO DO.
PERHAPS I NEED A PAL WHO NEEDS ME TOO.

FARMER ED KNEW WHY LUCKY WAS SO SAD.
HE KNEW WHAT WOULD MAKE LUCKY VERY GLAD.
HE SAID, STEP INTO THE BARN. I'VE SOMETHING YOU SHOULD SEE.
YOU CAN RIDE TONY THE PONY 'CAUSE HE'S TOO SMALL FOR ME.

TAKE TONY THE PONY TO THE PASTURE OUT BACK.
TAKE HIM FOR A RIDE; WHEN YOU ARE TIRED, BRING HIM BACK.
LET HIM RUN THE PASTURE WITH HIS HEAD BACK IN THE WIND.
LUCKY, I PROMISE YOU, YOU'LL BE HIS BEST FRIEND.

LET THE OTHER CHILDREN COME AND RIDE HIM EVERY DAY.
YOU HAVE THE ONLY PONY: YOU CAN MAKE THEM PAY.
FRIENDS WILL COME TO SEE YOU, WITH YOU, THEY'LL WANT TO PLAY.
THEY WILL RIDE TONY THE PONY: THEY WILL RIDE HIM EVERY DAY.

WILL YOU COME AND FEED YOUR ANIMAL
FRIENDS AND FEED THEM EVERY DAY?
MRS WELCH WILL BAKE YOU COOKIES. THEN
YOU AND TONY CAN GO AND PLAY.

YES, FARMER ED, I WILL FEED THEM
EVERY DAY, AND THEN I'LL GO AND PLAY.
I'LL PLAY WITH ALL THE ANIMALS AND
BRING THEM TO YOUR BARN TO STAY.
I WILL TAKE TONY THE PONY, AND TO THE
PASTURE, WE WILL RIDE AWAY.

LUCKY RIDES TONY IN THE PASTURE. THEY ARE GETTING ALONG VERY WELL.
LUCKY SPOTS A GIRL LOOKING AND WATCHING FROM OUTSIDE THE FENCE RAIL.
SHE IS SMILING, WITH RED HAIR UNDER A STRAW HAT AND VERY SHORT PIGTAILS.

LUCKY RIDES TONY DOWN THE HILL
TO GET A BETTER VIEW.
SHE SAID MY NAME IS GINGER, AND
I'VE BEEN WATCHING YOU.
LUCKY TOLD TONY, BE NICE TO
GINGER, AND LET HER RIDE ON YOU.
WE'LL ALL GO OVER TO MRS WELCH'S;
SHE'LL GIVE US A COOKIE OR TWO.

THIS IS FARMER ED AND HIS WIFE, MRS WELCH, AND THIS IS THEIR FARM.
I WANT TO INTRODUCE YOU TO MY ANIMAL FRIENDS, LIVING IN THE BARN.

THIS IS EINSWINE, THE PIG, AND TOAT, THE GOAT,
WHO IS STARING AT YOU.
YOU CAN FEED THEM SOME SWEET CORN, BUT ONLY
A SCOOP OR TWO.

I HAVE A BEAGLE NAMED DAISY: I'M SURE
SHE WILL LIKE YOU.
WE CAN PLAY WITH HER UNTIL A RABBIT
SHE SEES IF YOU WANT TO.

MRS WELCH GIVES THEM ALL COOKIES WITH A KISS AND A HUG.
I WILL GO AND GET SOME FRESH MILK, SOME GLASSES AND A JUG.

LUCKY, I HAVE TO GO HOME NOW. FROM HERE I DON'T LIVE FAR.
I HAD SO MUCH FUN TODAY: I'LL COME BACK AND PLAY TOMORROW.
I HAVE TO GO HOME AND PRACTICE: I'M LEARNING TO PLAY THE GUITAR.

LUCKY SITS DOWN TO WATCH FARMER ED,
WHO IS STACKING HAY.
FARMER ED, ASK LUCKY, TELL ME, WHAT
DID YOU LEARN TODAY?

DAISY THE BEAGLE LOVES TO PLAY AND BE MY BEST FRIEND.
SHE LOVES TO RUN THE SAME RABBIT OVER AND OVER AGAIN.

TOAT THE GOAT, HE LOVES TO EAT TREES,
BUSHES, AND WEEDS.
I UNDERSTAND HE IS A GOAT, AND
CHEWING IS WHAT HE NEEDS.

EINSWINE THE PIG, IN THE PASTURE, FOR ROOTS, SHE LOVES TO DIG.
SHE EATS EVERYTHING BELOW THE GROUND, BUT THEN, SHE IS A PIG.

TONY THE PONY, WHO ME AND MY
FRIENDS LOVE TO RIDE AND PLAY.
THEN HE GETS TIRED AFTER A WHILE, AND
HE JUST WANTS TO EAT HAY.

MRS WELCH SHE IS A LOVELY SOUL: SHE LOVES TO COOK AND BAKE.
AND FARMER ED, SO KIND TO EVERYONE, A GREAT FRIEND YOU MAKE.

GINGER, MY NEW NEIGHBOR FRIEND, WITH HER I LOVE TO PLAY.
BUT SHE HAS TO GO HOME AND PRACTICE HER GUITAR EVERY DAY.

I UNDERSTAND NOW THAT WE ALL HAVE THINGS THAT WE LOVE TO DO.
I ENJOY PLAYING WITH EVERYONE, AND I WANT THEM TO HAVE FUN TOO.
I ACCEPT THEM ALL FOR WHO THEY ARE AND WHAT THEY HAVE TO GIVE.
WE ALL HELP EACH OTHER HERE AND ON THIS FARM...

WE HAPPILY WILL LIVE.

www.ingramcontent.com/pod-product-compliance
Lightning Source LLC
Chambersburg PA
CBHW041729100726
47973CB00010B/158

9798330566860